# Mr. Putter and Tabby
# Fly the Plane

CYNTHIA RYLANT

# Mr. Putter and Tabby
# Fly the Plane

Illustrated by
ARTHUR HOWARD

SCHOLASTIC INC.
New York  Toronto  London  Auckland  Sydney

ISBN 0-590-33052-7

Text copyright © 1997 by Cynthia Rylant.
Illustrations copyright © 1997 by Arthur Howard.
All rights reserved. Published by Scholastic Inc., 555 Broadway, New York, NY 10012,
by arrangement with Harcourt Brace & Company.

SCHOLASTIC and associated logos are trademarks and/or registered trademarks of
Scholastic Inc.

12 11 10 9 8 7 6 5 4 3          9/9 0 1 2/0

Printed in the U.S.A.          23
First Scholastic printing, October 1997

For Kaitlin Dean, even newer
— C. R.

For Sophia Elizabeth Howard
— A. H.

# Mr. Putter and Tabby
# Fly the Plane

# 1

# Toys

Mr. Putter loved toys.
He was old, and he knew
that he wasn't supposed
to love toys anymore.
But he did.
When Mr. Putter and his
fine cat, Tabby, drove into town,
they always stopped at the toy store.

Tabby was not happy at the toy store.
She was old, too,
and her nerves weren't as good
as they used to be.

The wind-ups made her twitch.
The pop-ups made her jump.
And anything that flew
gave her the hiccups.

But Tabby loved Mr. Putter,
so she put up with all of it.
While she twitched and jumped
and hiccuped, Mr. Putter
played with everything.

He played with the dump trucks.

He played with the cranes.

He played with the bear on the
flying trapeze.

But most of all,
he played with the planes.

Ever since he was a boy
Mr. Putter had loved planes.
When he was young he had covered
his whole room with them.
Biplanes were his favorite,
but he also loved monoplanes
and seaplanes
and shiny ace Junkers.

He thought he might really fly
a plane one day.
But he never did.
So now he just looked at toy planes
every chance he got.

One day when
Mr. Putter and Tabby
were in the toy store and Tabby
was hissing at a wind-up penguin,
Mr. Putter spotted a plane
he had never seen before.

It was white and red, with
two wings on each side
and a little flag on its tail.
It was the most beautiful biplane
he had ever seen.
And it had a radio control
so a person might really fly it.

Mr. Putter was in love.

He bought the little plane and put it
in the car with Tabby.

He told her not to worry.

He promised her a nice cup of tea
with lots of cream
and a warm English muffin.

But still she hiccuped all the way home.

# 2

# The Little Plane

Mr. Putter kept his promise.
He gave Tabby tea with cream
and a warm English muffin.
Then together they went outside
to fly his new plane.

Tabby had stopped hiccuping,
but only because she was full of tea.
She still didn't like Mr. Putter's plane.
Mr. Putter sat on the grass
and read all the directions.

Then he put the plane on the grass
and stepped back
and pressed the start button.
But the plane did not start.
It just rolled over and died.
Tabby purred.

Mr. Putter ran to the little plane.

He set it right again.

He told it to be a good little plane.

He stepped back

and pressed the start button.

But the plane did not start.

It fell on its nose and died.

Tabby purred and purred.

Mr. Putter ran to the plane.

He brushed the dirt off its nose.

He told it to be a brave little plane.

He stepped back

and pressed the start button.

But the plane did not start.

One of its wings fell off

and it died.

Tabby purred and purred and purred.

But poor Mr. Putter was so sad.

He picked up his little biplane.

He told the plane that it was all his fault.

He told it that he was an old man

and old men shouldn't have toys anyway.

He said he wasn't any good at flying planes.

Tabby watched Mr. Putter.

She could see that he was sad.

Then she felt sad, too.

Tabby went to Mr. Putter
and rubbed herself against his legs.
She sat on his shoulder,
put her head by his,
and licked his nose.
This made Mr. Putter feel better.

He decided to try again.

He fixed the wing.

He set the little plane on the grass.

He told it that he and Tabby knew

it was the best plane in the world.

Then he pressed the start button.

The little plane choked.

The little plane coughed.

The little plane gagged.

But it didn't die.

It warmed up and began to sound better.

Then slowly, slowly,

it rolled across the grass.

It picked up speed. . . .

And then it *flew*!

It flew high into the blue sky.

Mr. Putter cheered.

Tabby purred and hiccuped.

Mr. Putter was finally flying
a plane of his own!

# 3

# The Boy

Every day for many weeks
Mr. Putter and Tabby flew
the little biplane.

Tabby never hiccuped anymore.
She had become used to flying things.
Children from town
heard about the plane,
and they all came to the fields
to watch it fly.

Mr. Putter loved this.

He liked the company.

He let the children take turns

flying the little plane, and he

felt like a proud grandpa.

One boy he liked best of all.
The boy was a little shy,
a little clumsy,
a little forgetful.
Just like Mr. Putter.
But whenever the boy flew
Mr. Putter's plane, he wasn't
shy or clumsy or forgetful at all.
He was strong.
He was sure.
He was happy.

When Mr. Putter saw this,
he remembered himself as a boy.
He remembered how he had wanted
a plane that really flew.
He remembered lying awake every night
wishing for one.

Now Mr. Putter had his plane.

But he was old.

He didn't need it as much.

He had Tabby and she was
everything he needed.

So one day he gave his little biplane
to the shy, clumsy, forgetful boy.
The boy became a hero
among the other children.

And Mr. Putter and Tabby went back
to their tea and muffins,
their tulips and roses,

their morning naps and
afternoon puddings.

And sometimes, when they were
out for a walk together,

a proud little biplane
flew high above their heads.

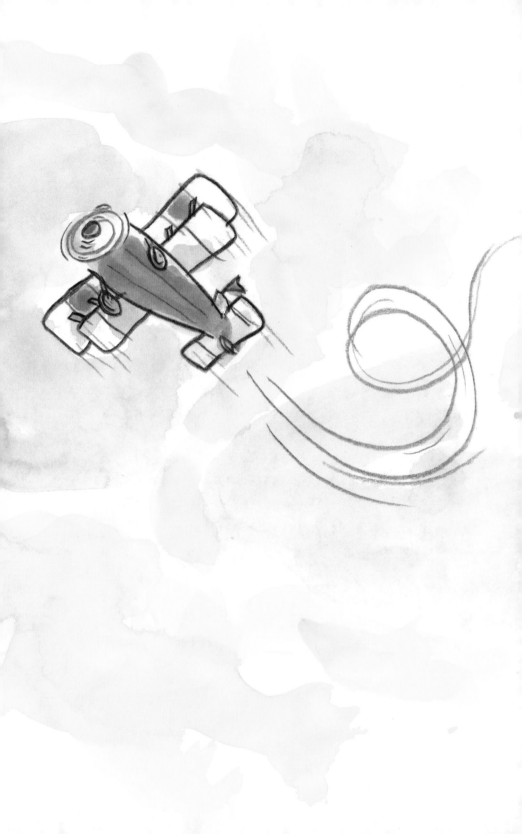

The illustrations in this book were done in pencil, watercolor,
gouache, and Sennelier pastels on 90-pound vellum paper.
The display type was set in Artcraft and the
text type was set in Berkeley Old Style Book.
Color separations were made by United Graphic Pte Ltd., Singapore.

Designed by Arthur Howard and Carolyn Stafford